10 9 8 7 6 5 4 3 2 1 · 17 18 19 20 21
Printed in China 38
First edition, September 2017
The text type was set in Irish Grover.
Book design by Patti Ann Harris

For Scary McDylan
—R.L.S.

For Liza and Patti Ann
—M.B.

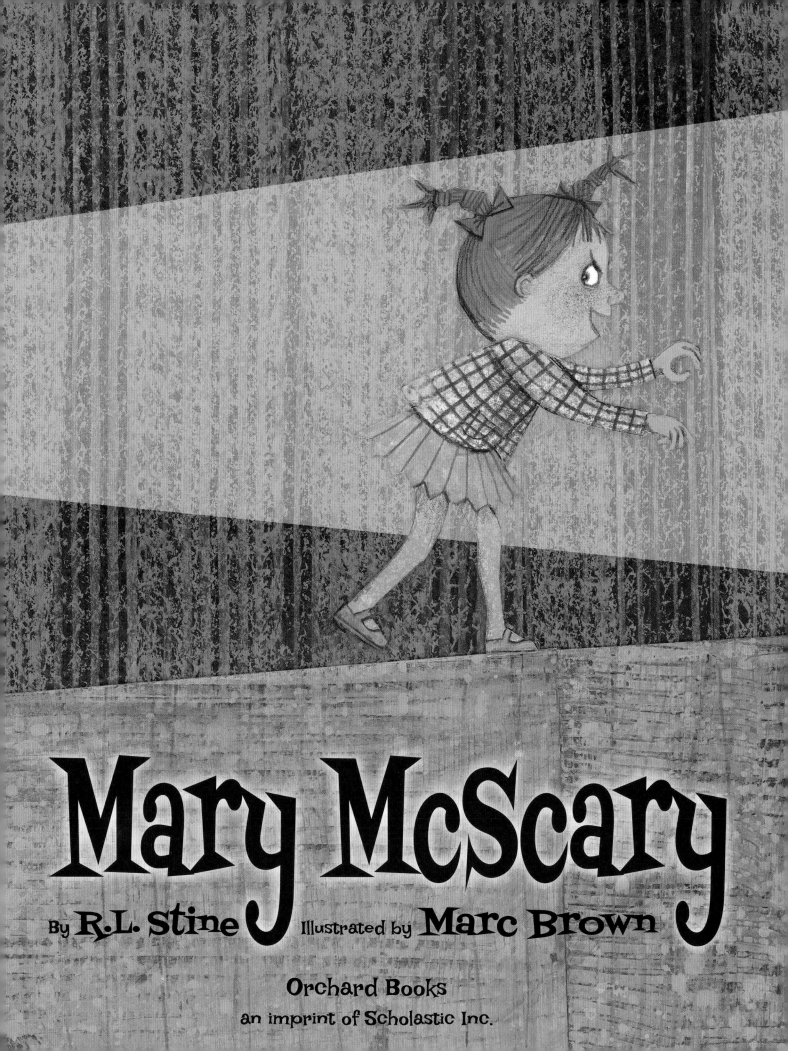

Mary McScary

By R.L. Stine   Illustrated by Marc Brown

Orchard Books

an imprint of Scholastic Inc.

Meet Mary McScary.
She likes to be scary.
She doesn't shout BOO!
She shouts . . .

Beware of Mary McScary!

Mary scares her dad
at breakfast.

Mary scares her mom
at lunch.

Is Mary scary at dinner?
You betcha!

Beware of Mary McScary!

Mary McScary
has fun
scaring dogs.

She likes
to scare
goldfish, too.

Mary's so scary, she can scare a **BALLOON!**

Beware of Mary McScary!

Mary can scare just about everyone . . .

EXCEPT Harry McScary.
Harry is Mary McScary's cousin.
Harry is coming to visit.
Harry does NOT find Mary scary.
WILL MARY SCARE HARRY?

"Today is the day I will
finally scare Harry.
I can't wait to make him **SCREAM!**"

Mary gets ready.
She puts on her scariest,
hairiest costume.

"Nice hairdo, Mary!"

She opens the door with a
RRROOOAAARRRRR!
But Harry's not scared of Mary.

Mary McScary
tries again.
Maybe giant spiders
will scare Harry!

"LOOK OUT!
Giant spiders!"

"Awwww,
I love spiders!
So cute
and cuddly!"

"Hmph!
I'll show you
something
scary, Harry!"

"Watch out! GORILLA!
Wild and ferocious gorilla!"

"WHEEEEEEEEE

Mary McScary
knew this
just wouldn't do.

"I know!
Slippery, slimy snakes for Harry.
Now THAT'S scary!"

"You guys give the best hugs!"

HELP!

"I'm being eaten by a GIANT HUNGRY hippo!"

"Cootchie-cootchie-coo!
I could tickle a hippo all day!"

"I GIVE UP!"

"**BUT WAIT!**
There's only
one thing
left to do . . ."

"You win,
Harry McScary!
Nothing scares you."
She turns to kiss him . . .

EEEEEEEE EEEEEK!

"I told you I was scary!
Beware of Mary McScary!"